ABC GULLS

By Beth Rand

ISLANDPORT PRESS

Text and illustrations © 2017 by Beth Rand

Published by Islandport Press
P.O. Box 10
Yarmouth, Maine 04096
books@islandportpress.com
www.islandportpress.com

ISBN: 978-1-944762-08-7
Library of Congress Control Number:
2016957654
Printed in USA by Versa Press

For Jeff, my island companion, and for Charlie, the gull chaser who never gives up.

Airplane

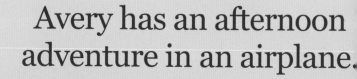

Avery has an afternoon
adventure in an airplane.

Bailey balances on the bow of a beautiful boat.

Boat

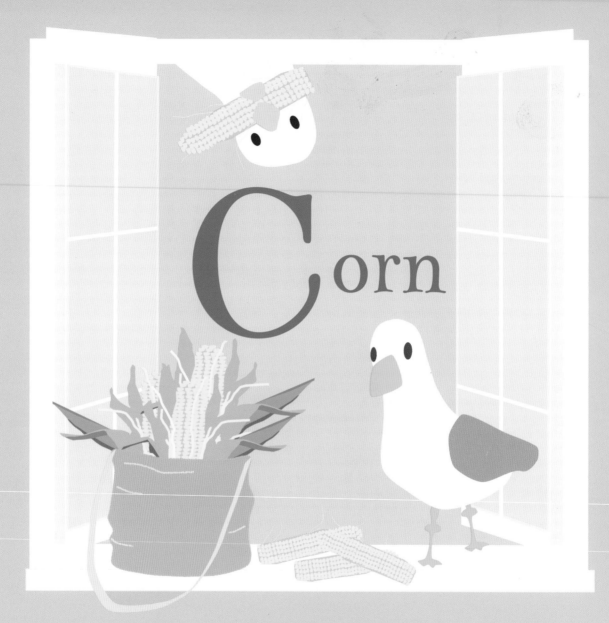

Corn

Cliff and Cushing are content to spot cobs of corn on the counter.

Dog

Dodge is determined to ride on the dog,
all the way to the dock.

Emery
excitedly
orbits the
earth.

Earth

Fish

Folly finally catches the feisty fish.

Grill

Griffin gets the grill going.

Hike

Haskell hits the trail and heads off on a hike.

Island

The Ivy twins float to the island in inner tubes. What a day!

Jump

Jewell enjoys a refreshing jump off the jetty.

Kite

Keeler gets a kick out of flying a kite at the park.

Lobster

Ledge loves to see lobsters in his trap.

Moxie marvels at meeting a magical mermaid.

Mermaid

Nest

Nubble notices new eggs in the nest.

Owl

Otter opts to stay up
overnight with an owl.

Pumpkin

Preble and
Pudding
prefer the
pumpkin
patch.

Queen

The sandcastle makes Quoddy feel like a queen.

Ripley and friends relax on a roof in the rain.

Roof

Schoodic
sneaks away
after stealing
a sandwich.

Sandwich

Tugboat

Tibbetts takes a trip around town in a tugboat.

Umpire

Unfortunately, it's not Upton's day at the plate.
Umpire says, "You're out!"

Volleyball

Vaill and Varney value their vacation
playing volleyball.

Whale

Webber takes a wild ride in the spout of a whale

X-ray

Xander examines his x-ray. Oh, no!

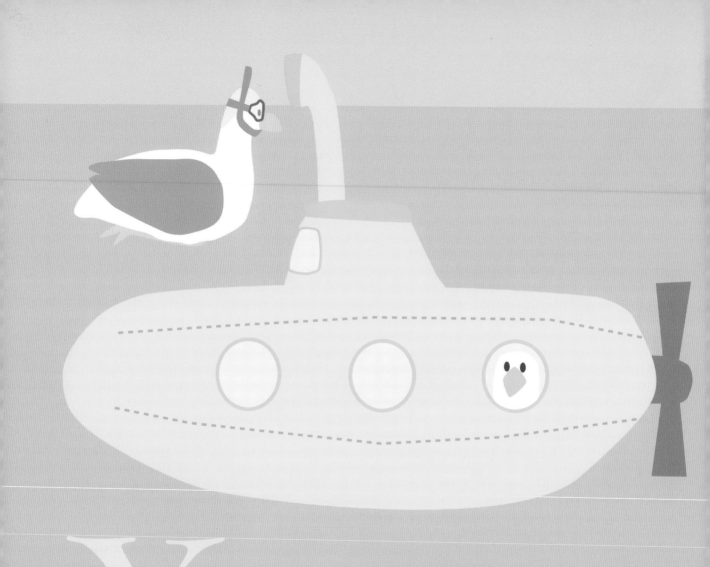

Yellow

York says, "Yikes! A yellow submarine!"

Zipper

Zeke pulls up
his zipper.
He's ready to
zoom off to
Zephyr Cove.

About the Author

Photo by Kevin Bennett

Beth Rand is a self-taught illustrator who has published her own line of greeting cards and a poster calendar featuring Maine imagery. *ABC Gulls* is her first children's picture book.

Born in Pittsburgh, Pennsylvania, having a Navy dentist for a dad meant that Rand had an itinerant childhood, moving from Maryland to Rhode Island to South Carolina and even Sicily. Since graduating from the University of Maine, she has made Maine her home. For twenty years, she and her husband lived in Cape Elizabeth, where they successfully raised three children to adulthood. Then they hopped on the ferry to Peaks Island, and never looked back. Rand now lives on the island with her husband and dog, in a home surrounded by seagulls, sunshine, and salt air. When foul weather keeps her inside, illustration becomes the focus.

Author's Note

You might notice that the seagulls have unusual names. There's a reason for that! In my home state of Maine there are more than 3,000 islands. Seagulls probably visit all of them. I thought it would be fun to name the seagulls after as many Maine islands as possible. Some are big, and have towns with people and cars on them, while some are just chunks of rocks. No island names start with the letters Q, U, or X, though, so those names are just for fun!